Sweet
Secrets

READ ALL THE CANDY FAIRIES BOOKS!

Chocolate Dreams

Rainbow Swirl

Caramel Moon

Cool Mint

Magic Hearts

Gooey Goblins

The Sugar Ball

A Valentine's Surprise

Bubble Gum Rescue

Double Dip

Jelly Bean Jumble

The Chocolate Rose

A Royal Wedding

Marshmallow Mystery

Frozen Treats

The Sugar Cup

COMING SOON:

Taffy Trouble

Candy Fairies

Sweet Secrets

HELEN PERELMAN

ILLUSTRATED BY
ERICA-JANE WATERS

ALADDIN
NEW YORK LONDON TORONTO SYDNEY NEW DELHI

ALADDIN

An imprint of Simon & Schuster Children's Publishing Division

1230 Avenue of the Americas, New York, New York 10020

This Aladdin paperback edition January 2015

Text copyright © 2015 by Helen Perelman Bernstein

Illustrations copyright © 2015 by Erica-Jane Waters

Also available in an Aladdin hardcover edition.

All rights reserved, including the right of reproduction in whole or in part in any form.

ALADDIN is a trademark of Simon & Schuster, Inc., and related logo
is a registered trademark of Simon & Schuster, Inc.

For information about special discounts for bulk purchases, please contact
Simon & Schuster Special Sales at 1-866-506-1949 or business@simonandschuster.com.

The Simon & Schuster Speakers Bureau can bring authors to your live event.
For more information or to book an event contact the Simon & Schuster Speakers Bureau
at 1-866-248-3049 or visit our website at www.simonspeakers.com.

Book design by Karina Granda

The text of this book was set in Baskerville Book.

Manufactured in the United States of America 1214 OFF

2 4 6 8 10 9 7 5 3 1

Library of Congress Control Number 2014953628

ISBN 978-1-4814-0611-6 (hc)

ISBN 978-1-4814-0610-9 (pbk)

ISBN 978-1-4814-0612-3 (eBook)

For Grandma Ellie,
stylish and sweet!

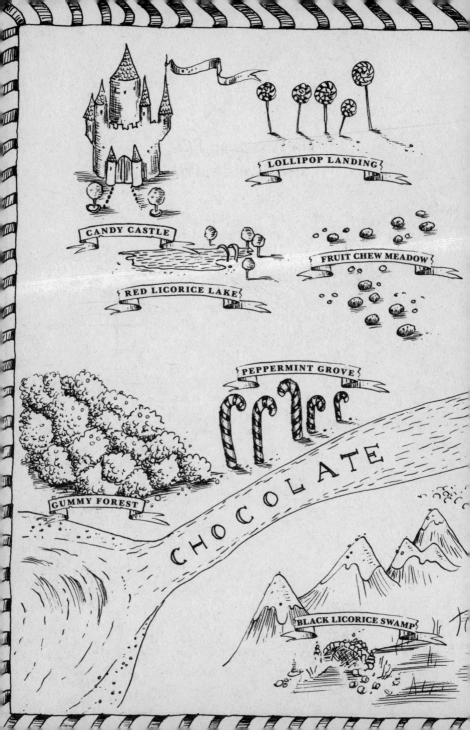

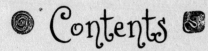 Contents

CHAPTER

1

Supersweet News

Berry the Fruit Fairy headed to Red Licorice Lake at top speed. She wasn't racing to Sun Dip because she was late. Usually she did arrive at the red sugar sand beach at Red Licorice Lake just as the sun was starting to slide behind the Frosted Mountains. Sun Dip was the time that her Candy Fairy friends

1

shared stories and sweets. Her friends knew Berry was always the last to arrive. But today was different. Berry fluttered her wings faster. Today Berry was rushing to get there early because she was about to burst with her good news!

There was no one she wanted to share her news with more than her best friends.

"Wow! Berry, you are so early!" Raina the Gummy Fairy exclaimed when she saw Berry.

"Hot caramel, what's wrong?" Melli gasped. She was spreading her blanket out on the sand and stood up with a concerned look. The dark-haired Caramel Fairy looked worried. "Berry, you are never early. Is everything all right?"

"Something must be wrong," Cocoa the Chocolate Fairy added as she arrived. She turned to Berry. "Are you okay?"

"She looks too good to be in trouble," Dash said from above. The small Mint Fairy eyed her well-dressed friend. She landed next to Berry and looked her up and down, from her sugarcoated fruit hair clips to her sparkly sugar shoes.

If Berry wasn't so happy, she might have gotten steamed up, but instead she just laughed. "Very funny," she said. "I have super-sweet news!"

"Well, go ahead!" Raina told her. "We're all here."

Berry took a deep breath. Her heart was racing so fast! "I have been invited to enter the Meringue Island Fashion Show for Young Fairies," she blurted out. She floated above the red sugar sand. She couldn't keep her wings still! "I sent in drawings for the past two years and I have finally been asked to be part of the competition!"

"Isn't Olivia Crème de la Crème judging this year?" Raina asked.

Berry nodded quickly. "Yes! How sweet is that?"

Raina leaped up to give Berry a tight squeeze.

"Oh, Olivia is the best designer on Meringue Island," Cocoa sighed. She opened up her basket full of Sun Dip treats. "This calls for some chocolate celebration. And I happen to have some! I made these chocolate sprinkle balls this afternoon. Have some!"

"Hmm, remember the sweet treats we got when we were getting fitted for our gumdrop dresses for Princess Lolli's wedding?" Dash said wistfully. She popped a chocolate in her mouth. "I love Meringue Island, and especially Sweet Stitches."

Berry clapped her hands. "Yes!" she exclaimed. "The event is at Olivia's store! She is going to set up a huge tent behind her store for the show. She is making a runway for the models, just like in one of her fashion shows!"

"This competition has been going on for many years," Raina said. "In the Fairy Code Book there's a story about when Olivia Crème de la Crème won it as a young fairy."

Berry smiled at Raina. No one knew the Fairy Code Book better than her friend. "I knew that sweet fact," she said.

"Well, she definitely made Princess Lolli the most scrumptious wedding dress," Melli said. "Plus, Olivia Crème de la Crème was very nice."

"Oh, Olivia is the berriest!" Berry exclaimed. She took the invitation out of her bag to show her friends. "I don't remember the Sweet Stitches treats like Dash does, but I do remember Olivia's designs!"

Cocoa took the invitation. "This is perfect for you," she said, reading the card. "And look at this card! It is *sugar-tastic!*"

Berry had spent the day admiring the beautiful paper and artwork on the invitation. She took it back and put it in the envelope. All the colors were so beautiful and reminded Berry of Lollipop Landing when all the lollipops were ripe. Nothing Olivia Crème de la Crème did was in bad taste.

"You've been dreaming of a chance to show off your designs, and this is the sweetest way!" Cocoa said. "Imagine all the attention your design will get!"

"Meringue Island is the fashion capital of Sugar Valley!" Melli added. "This is supersweet news."

"I've always loved this event," Berry sighed. "I would read about it in the *Daily Scoop* and imagine my own designs being judged." She sat down on the blanket next to Dash. The sun was nearing the Frosted Mountains and the sky was a beautiful pattern of pastels. "This is the most gorgeous Sun Dip! And the sweetest day ever!"

"How many fairies were invited?" Melli asked.

"There were twelve invitations sent," Berry said. "I am not sure who else got an invite, but I know Fruli did. Her family is running the whole show."

Fruli was a fancy Fruit Fairy from Meringue Island who worked in Fruit Chew Meadow with Berry. When Berry first met Fruli, she thought that the fancy fairy was snobby and sour. Berry was often jealous of

Fruli and all her clothes and her fancy house. Fruli turned out to be nothing like Berry had imagined, and she was a good friend to all the Candy Fairies.

"Can I see the invitation?" Raina asked.

Berry handed it to her. When she did, a piece of paper fell out of the envelope.

Raina picked it up. "Did you see this?" she asked, unfolding the small note. "This year's competition has a twist."

"A twist?" Berry mumbled. Her mouth was full of Cocoa's chocolate sprinkle drops.

"I guess you didn't see these rules?" Raina asked.

She pointed to the small piece of raspberry-colored paper.

"What rules?" Berry asked, flying over.

"Of course Raina would read all the fine print," Dash said with a giggle. "She'll read anything!"

"It's a good thing I do read everything," Raina scoffed. "Berry, the competition is different this year. I guess that is why there is a special card in the envelope to explain. This year you don't have all weekend to prepare an outfit. You will only have an hour to make your outfit—and the fabric is a surprise!"

"Huh," Berry said. She took the small card back. "I didn't notice that piece of paper." She studied the new rules. She made a face as she realized that this year the fashion contest was going to be more challenging than in the past.

"Sounds like more of a race than a design show," Cocoa said.

"So mint!" Dash said, rubbing her hands together. "I guess Olivia Crème de la Crème is trying to keep it all fresh."

Berry narrowed her eyes. She had waited so long to be invited to participate in the fashion event, and now, with these changes, she wasn't sure she'd be up to the challenge. "This is going to be one sticky fashion show," she told her friends.

CHAPTER 2

New Rules

Berry slumped down on Melli's blanket. She let her fingers sink into the soft red sand. This was turning out to be the saddest Sun Dip. She had thought tonight would be a celebration. The news that the competition would be different and much harder than she had expected was not making her feel like celebrating at all. She kept rereading the raspberry note. How could she have missed seeing that piece of paper?

"This is definitely not going to be a typical design competition," Berry said with a sour face.

"Aw, cheer up, Berry," Cocoa said. "Maybe it will be fun!"

Dash smiled at Berry. "Aren't you the one to always say 'Don't dip your wings in syrup yet'?"

Berry gave Dash a cold stare. "Well, I just got a bucket of syrup dumped on me," she grumbled.

Raina leaned in closer to Berry. "Dash is right," she said. "I know this may seem a little tough, but not everything is ruined."

"You still got invited to be in the contest," Melli said. "That's an honor."

Berry knew her friends were trying to help, but she was feeling crushed. "I wish I had been invited last year, when everyone got to pick their own fabrics and stayed at the design studio for the weekend. I heard all the fairies had a blast."

"Double minty," Dash said. "You don't get much time to plan out your design when you find out the material."

"Bittersweet," Cocoa added. "What if you get some sticky, tacky material? What would you do?"

"Cocoa," Raina muttered, waving her hand for her to stop talking.

"Don't you still get to stay at Olivia's studio for the night?" Melli asked.

Berry pulled her knees up to her chest.

"Yes, but the design part is cut short. What if I can't work with the surprise material or think of a *sweet-tacular* design?"

"I'm sure that you'll be able to come up with something," Cocoa said, trying to sound convincing.

"And there's no rule about your friends not going with you," Raina said, smiling. "Let's all go to Meringue Island!"

"Sure as sugar!" Dash cheered. "We can be the best design cheering squad."

"Hold on," Berry said. "It's not like you can all take Butterscotch."

Butterscotch was the Candy Castle unicorn who had given the Candy Fairies a ride the last time they'd gone to Meringue Island, for a dress fitting for Princess Lolli's wedding.

"There are only rides for the contestants. And you can't sail the Vanilla Sea like we did during the warmer months," Berry said. She looked at her friends. "Where would you stay? All the contestants stay at Sweet Stitches."

Melli nodded. "You're right," she said. "But we'll think of something." She moved closer to Berry. "Don't you want us to come?"

Berry looked at her friends. "Sweet strawberries, of course I want you to come," she replied. She wanted them to come more than she could express. Having her friends by her side would make the competition sweeter.

"We could see if we can stay at Fruli's," Raina suggested.

Berry nodded. "Fruli will be there. I am sure she'd let you stay at her house."

"I would love to stay in Fruli's palace again," Melli said with a sigh. "Remember when we stayed there for Dash and Cocoa's Double Dip race? All those luscious rooms and the views of Cone Harbor were delicious."

"Yes," Dash said, "and all those yummy treats." She sighed, rubbing her stomach.

"Dash, do you always think of food?" Melli said, laughing.

Dash flew up from her spot on the blanket and snapped her fingers. "Wait a minty minute! I've got a supersweet idea."

"Does it involve sweet treats?" Cocoa asked.

Dash floated back down to the ground. "No," she said, "but it does involve us getting to Meringue Island."

 19

Berry looked over at Dash. "How?" she asked.

"Carobee!" Dash shouted with glee. "We haven't seen that dragon in a while. Wouldn't it be fun to see him again? He'd give us a lift to Meringue Island!"

"Sweet sugars!" Raina exclaimed. "That is a sweet idea, Dash. What do you say, Berry?"

"That would be *sugar-tastic!*" Berry exclaimed. "Do you think Carobee would do it?"

"Let's send a sugar fly note to Carobee now," Cocoa said. She wrote a quick letter and waved down a sugar fly. "You'll find Carobee in Sugar Cove in the Candy Cliffs," she said, handing the note to the fly.

"Don't worry, Berry," Raina said. "You are going to pull this off. I doubt that any fairy wants this win more than you."

"But that doesn't mean I'll win," Berry said, looking down at the sand.

"You will definitely have fun," Cocoa said, swinging her arm around Berry. "You've got the best team of supporters this side of the Frosted Mountains."

While Berry wasn't sure how she could prepare or plan for the surprise fabric that she would have to sew, she knew her friends would be there with her. She hoped that Carobee would answer quickly and they could all start packing for the big event.

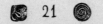

CHAPTER 3

Fruli's Secret

For the next few days Berry spent her time poring over fashion magazines and her design notebook. She wanted to memorize different patterns and styles to help her during the competition. Not knowing the fabric was going to make the hour of design time stressful. Berry wanted to be prepared.

"Berry, what are you doing?" Raina asked as she flew over Lollipop Landing. "You didn't come to Gummy Forest yesterday or today. I need some fruit flavor sprinkles for the gummy fish." She settled down next to Berry. "And I'm a little worried about you." Raina looked at all the papers surrounding Berry. "Why so many crumpled-up pieces of paper?" she asked.

Berry sighed. She ripped up the piece of paper she was drawing on. "It's no use," she moaned. "I can't design anything!" She threw her chocolate sketching chalk down. "How will I be able to design and sew a winning dress in just an hour? And how will I manage with a material that I may have never used before?"

Raina sat down and smoothed out one of

23

Berry's drawings. "This one has possibilities," she said, admiring the sketch.

"You're just saying that to be nice," Berry mumbled.

"No," Raina said, "I mean it. And everyone in the competition has the same time to create and complete a dress. It will be a challenge for everyone." She smiled at her friend. "You love a good challenge!"

"Not anymore," Berry said. "Oh, Raina, I really want to win this! I've been dreaming of this fashion show for so long."

"Berry, you've got to snap out of this sour mood," Raina scolded. "You are so talented. I'll bet all the other fairies are nervous about competing with *you*."

Berry gathered up the drawings and

stuffed them into a bag. "I don't know about that," she said. "None of these designs would win the grand prize."

"Not true," Raina said.

"What happens if the material is fruit leather or a caramel flannel? Those materials are impossible to sew," Berry said.

Raina took a deep breath. "Don't get all worked up about the material. The important thing is to keep calm. You'll know what to do. I know you will."

Berry realized that Raina was going to have an answer for every worry she had. She smiled at her friend. She knew Raina was trying to help.

"Raina, would you be my model?" Berry asked.

"Really?" Raina asked.

Berry smiled. "You'd be perfect for the runway," she said. "And that way you'll be with me to keep me calm!"

Raina fluttered her wings. "It would be my honor! And superfun!" she cried.

"I was hoping you'd say that," Berry replied.

"Right now we've got to get going," Raina told her. "I'm here to make sure you come to Sun Dip. Fruli said she'd join us tonight. That should cheer you up."

Berry didn't really feel like going to Sun Dip. She didn't want to see perfect Fruli and have to be all perky and sweet.

"Has anyone heard back from Carobee?" Berry asked, changing the subject.

"I was hoping you might have news," Raina replied. "No one seems to know where he is. It's not like him to not respond to a sugar fly note. Maybe Cocoa has heard. Come on, it's almost time for Sun Dip. Let's go ask her."

Berry put her supplies away and followed Raina to Red Licorice Lake. She would try to be a bit less sour about the competition, but if Fruli went on and on about all the amazing designs in the shows from the last couple of years, she might burst!

Berry and Raina found Dash, Cocoa, Melli, and Fruli already gathered at the lake.

"Any word from Carobee?" Cocoa asked Berry and Raina when they arrived.

"We were hoping you might have news," Raina replied, shaking her head. "Fruli, have you heard any news about Carobee?"

"No," Fruli said. "But I haven't been on Meringue Island much these days. I've been working at Candy Kingdom on a project for Princess Lolli."

"Oh, really?" Raina asked. "What are you doing?"

Fruli blushed. "Oh, nothing much," she said. "I decided not to be in Olivia's design competition so I could do this special project instead."

"A *special* project?" Berry asked. She eyed her friend. "And you aren't going to be in the show?" Fruli loved fashion just as much as Berry did. Was Fruli hiding something?

Fruli shook her head. "No," she said. Then she glanced up and pointed to the sky. "Look, it's Princess Lolli!"

"Hello my sweets!" Princess Lolli soared above the fairies and swooped down to say hello. "Berry, I wanted to congratulate you on the invitation to compete in Olivia's design contest. We're all very proud of you."

Berry beamed. "Thank you," she said.

"I've heard that Olivia has made the contest a little more challenging this year." The princess smiled. "But I know you will do well. We all can't wait to see your design."

Me neither, thought Berry.

Princess Lolli seemed to give Fruli a special look, and Berry wondered what the two of them were working on together. Berry watched as Princess Lolli took Fruli aside.

"Isn't it strange that Fruli didn't accept the invitation to the competition?" Berry whis-

pered to Raina. "She loves fashion as much as I do. Why didn't she want to be a part of it?"

Raina thought for a moment. "Maybe she wanted to do something else."

"You mean the secret project with Princess

Lolli?" Berry said, watching Fruli smile and nod at Princess Lolli.

"Maybe," Raina said. "If you're wondering what they are up to, why don't you just ask?"

Berry shrugged. She didn't want to ask Fruli. If Fruli wanted to tell her, she would.

When Princess Lolli left, Cocoa gathered the fairies together. "Time is running out," she said. "Since we haven't heard back from Carobee, we need to make other plans to get to Meringue Island. The competition starts in two days."

"If you need help getting to Meringue Island, you should take my family's unicorn," Fruli said. "I will send for Puff." She looked over at Berry. "Why didn't you tell me you needed a ride?"

"It's not for me," Berry said quickly. "The others want to come to the event."

"A ride on Puff?" Dash asked. *"So mint!"*

Fruli laughed. "Honestly, it's no problem. And I'd love for you all to stay with me at my house." She smiled at the fairies.

Berry couldn't help thinking that Fruli was hiding something. She had to admit, it was nice of her to invite them all. But Berry still had to wonder why Fruli did not enter the contest.

"You're not going to be in the contest, but you are going home?" Raina asked. She glanced over at Berry. Berry knew her friend was also thinking that Fruli was acting strange.

"Um, yes. I am going to the show," Fruli said. "I just decided not to be *in* the show."

"Thank you very much," Dash said to Fruli. "You are supersweet to have us all."

"Let's check on Carobee when we get there," Cocoa added. "Maybe he never got the sugar fly note."

Berry gave her friends hugs. She was thrilled they would be at Meringue Island with her. Even though she felt Fruli was keeping secrets, she was going to try not to let that distract her. She had more important things to worry about.

4

Sweet Send-Off

Berry tightened the strap on her trunk. She checked her list and double-checked again. She didn't want to forget a thing! As she stood on the Gummy Forest dock, waiting for her ride to Meringue Island, she kept thinking of what she might have forgotten to bring to the design competition. Had she remembered the comb for straightening cotton candy? Had she packed all her caramel needles? If she didn't have the right tools for making the winning dress, she knew she would feel sour.

"Berry, you brought enough luggage for a month!" Raina exclaimed when she saw all the trunks and bags on the dock. "Are you sure Butterscotch can take all this for you?"

"I hope so," Berry said. She looked around at her luggage. "I want to have all my favorite sewing needles and pins with me. I don't want to be a fashion disaster!"

"You could never be a fashion disaster," Dash said. She eyed the luggage. "You don't travel light, Berry."

Cocoa and Melli flew up behind them.

Berry was happy that her friends had **all come** to see her off.

"We're here for a sweet send-off," **Melli** told her.

"We saw Razz loading up her unicorn earlier," Cocoa said. "I think she is the only other Candy Fairy in the competition. The other contestants are coming from different kingdoms, right?"

Berry sighed. "Yes, and yuck—of all the Fruit Fairies to be in the competition," she hissed. "Razz is so juicy."

Razz was a little older than Berry and often did not have nice things to say. One time she made Berry feel terrible about her white jelly beans. "Don't let Razz bother you," Raina said.

"I'll try," Berry replied.

"Your ride should be here soon," Melli told Berry. "And we'll meet you at Fruli's later tonight."

"Maybe when we get to Meringue Island we'll find out what is going on with Carobee," Cocoa said.

"I'm worried about him," Melli said.

"You worry about everything!" Dash exclaimed. "Maybe he's out having a grand adventure in those cool cove caves."

"Maybe," Melli said, looking doubtful.

"I can't wait to stay at Fruli's," Dash went on. "Supermint of Fruli to let us stay in her castle again."

Berry made a face. "It's not actually a castle," she mumbled.

"What's gotten your wings all jumpy about Fruli?" Cocoa asked.

Berry shrugged. She really didn't want to worry about Fruli, but she couldn't help herself! "What do you think she is working on with Princess Lolli?" She thought for a moment. "Do you think the project is why she decided not to be part of the fashion show?"

"Maybe she knew she wouldn't make the cut," Dash said.

Everyone turned to look at Dash.

"What?" Dash asked. Her face turned a bright shade of gummy-fish red. "I'm just asking. She didn't try out, right?"

"Are you forgetting who we are talking about here?" Berry asked. "Fruli has more clothes than I could ever hope to have. She knows a ton about fashion. And her family has been a part of the fashion show for years. If it weren't for Fruli's family, Olivia wouldn't be able to run the show."

"But that doesn't make Fruli the best designer," Melli said.

Berry thought back to when the competitors had first been announced. She didn't remember Fruli saying that she wanted to be a designer. Berry had been so focused on her own application that she didn't remember Fruli saying anything about herself. But because Fruli knew so much about clothes and fancy dresses, Berry had thought she would be a contestant.

"She's up to something," Berry said. "I

know it. What is this secret project she is working on with Princess Lolli?"

"She never said it was secret," Melli said thoughtfully.

"It's nice that she has something special with Princess Lolli," Raina told Berry.

Cocoa flew up off the ground. "Look, everyone, here comes Butterscotch!"

The large royal unicorn came swooping down from the sky. His wings caught the wind, and he gently glided down to the ground.

Berry gathered her things, and with the help of her friends, loaded up the unicorn's back.

"Everything fits!" Berry said. She felt relieved. "I only hope I didn't forget anything!"

Dash looked at all the bags. "I doubt that!" she exclaimed.

Raina put her arm around Berry. "If you think of anything before tonight, send a sugar fly note. We don't leave until later today."

Berry gave her friends a tight squeeze. "Thank you!" she said. "I have a meeting with Olivia Crème de la Crème, but I'll be back for our dinner at Fruli's."

Melli clapped her hands. "I can't wait to hear what you have to report!" she said.

"I can't wait to see what we have for dinner at Fruli's!" Dash exclaimed.

"Oh, Dash," Berry said. She laughed. "Have a good flight. And I'll see you later!"

Berry flew up to her seat on Butterscotch and waved to her friends. "Bye!" she cried as the powerful unicorn took flight. Butterscotch soared through the air and over the Vanilla Sea.

In a few moments Berry could barely see her friends waving. As Butterscotch flew, Berry tried not to think about Fruli and Princess Lolli. She should be reviewing her patterns and stitches!

Berry sighed and leaned against Butterscotch's back. So many thoughts were swirling in her head. When had Fruli decided not to be part of the competition? Why hadn't Fruli told her?

The beat of Butterscotch's wings calmed Berry, and she tried to relax. Soon she would be at Meringue Island and meeting the rest of the fairies in the competition. She had plenty of time to be nervous. She tried to be calm and enjoy the ride.

When Berry arrived at Sweet Stitches a little while later, two of Olivia's assistants came out to help her with her bags.

"Welcome," a fairy with glittery yellow wings said. "We hope you enjoy your stay here and have fun with the competition."

I'm here to win the competition, Berry thought. She looked over at the doors of the store. To her, those doors meant a new beginning, and she felt a tingle from the tips of her wings to her toes.

CHAPTER
5

Twelve Fairies

Berry stood in the waiting room of Sweet Stitches. She remembered being in the famous designer's store for her royal wedding gumdrop dress fitting. Being a gumdrop at Princess Lolli's wedding had been *sugartastic*! Olivia Crème de la Crème had created scrumptious dresses for Berry and her friends.

The dresses were cotton-candy pink, each with a special candy emblem sewn on the front of the dress. There was a chocolate chip one for Cocoa, a mint candy for Dash, a caramel for Melli, a gumdrop for Raina, and a sugarcoated fruit slice for Berry. Berry loved the attention each one of them had gotten from Olivia Crème de la Crème. The dresses had been made just for them. Now Berry was going to get a different kind of attention.

"Hey, Berry," Razz called from the white meringue couch in the corner of the room.

Berry waved. She didn't want the sour Fruit Fairy to ruin her moment.

"When did you get here?" Razz asked as she flew over to Berry.

"I just flew in," Berry said. She looked

around. She hoped there was one of Olivia's assistants around to help her check in for the contest. The less time she spent talking to Razz the better!

"Oh, I came earlier," Razz told her. "I wanted to get in early. Get a head start."

Berry knew better than to listen to Razz. She knew no one would be allowed to start before the contest began tomorrow. She was positive that Razz was trying to spook her. And Berry was not going to fall for anything like that.

"Good for you," Berry said. "I'm going to check in now."

"Maybe we'll be roommates," Razz said, a bit too loudly.

Berry hadn't considered that. She made a

quick wish not to room with Razz. She smiled and flew away without another word. Berry smiled to herself. At least for now she had avoided a Razz insult!

"Hello and welcome to the Meringue Island Fashion Show for Young Fairies," a fairy said to Berry. The fairy looked down at her list. "What is your name and kingdom?"

"I am Berry from Candy Kingdom," Berry said proudly.

The fairy handed her a fabric folder with beautiful trim. "You were a gumdrop in Princess Lolli's wedding, weren't you?" she asked.

Berry blushed. "Yes, I was," she said.

The fairy smiled at her. "Welcome," she said. "In the folder is the information about the contest and your room assignment. Each contestant has her own room upstairs."

Berry breathed a sigh of relief. She didn't have to room with Razz!

"Please sit down and we'll start soon," the fairy said to Berry.

"Thank you," Berry said. She cradled the beautiful folder in her arms.

Just as Berry sat down, Olivia Crème de la Crème walked into the room. There were several gasps. Seeing a famous designer up close was very exciting for all the fairy contestants.

"Welcome!" Olivia said to the fairies. She was wearing a beautiful red licorice swirl skirt with a pale cotton-candy top. She looked as if she were walking on the runway in a fashion show. "We are thrilled to start the fashion event of the year!"

There was a big cheer. Berry sat up a little straighter. She was so happy to be a part of all this!

"You twelve fairies should feel very proud to have made it here this year," Olivia went on. Her sparkling wings fluttered. "There were many applications, and we had a hard time keeping the number down to just twelve." She smiled at Berry. "It is nice to see some new faces and some old faces here in the shop," she went on. "When I was a young fairy, I won the Meringue Island Fashion Show for Young Fairies. It is very nice for me to judge the contest this year. We made the event more challenging, but your applications were so outstanding we thought you could handle it."

Berry squeezed her hands together. She wasn't sure she was ready for all the new challenges.

"I trust you have all read the rules that were included with the invitation," Olivia said. "And in your packets, there is more information. Tomorrow is a big day. Please rest tonight, and tomorrow afternoon you can set up your workstations. Then it will be sew time!"

Berry was relieved that she could leave Sweet Stitches and see her friends at Fruli's. She waved quickly to Razz and flew out the door.

Fruli's home was as grand as she remembered. Dash was right—Fruli's house was like a palace. The fairy's great-grandparents had built it many years ago. There were several large rooms and a wide terrace overlooking Cone Harbor. Berry found her friends on the terrace.

"I'm so glad you made it here," she said. "How was your trip on Fluff?"

"*So mint!*" Dash replied. "We got here quickly. Unicorn travel is the best!"

"How was the sign-in?" Raina asked Berry.

"It was a little scary," Berry said. "There are twelve fairies in the contest. Razz was there, of course."

"Well, don't let that get you all ruffled," Melli said. "You need to focus on your design."

Berry nodded. "I will," she said. She looked around. "Where is Fruli? I thought she'd be here. Weren't we all going to eat together tonight?"

"Fruli had to fly off," Dash said. She was eating some tiny meringues from a large serving platter and lounging on a chair.

"See, she's up to something," Berry said.

 55

Raina shrugged. "Maybe," she said thoughtfully. "But she did arrange for a unicorn to take us tomorrow morning to find Carobee."

"Can you come with us?" Cocoa asked. "What time do you have to be at Sweet Stitches?"

Berry opened her folder. Inside was a schedule written on lemon-peel paper. "I don't need to be there until after lunch tomorrow," she said. She held up the schedule.

"Sweet sugars," Raina said, looking at the paper. "This is beautiful."

"And that is only the paper that the schedule is written on," Melli sighed. "What will the material be that you get tomorrow for the dress?"

Berry groaned and leaned back on the couch next to Dash. "I don't want to think about that now," she said. "But I do have to wonder where Fruli is. Don't you think it is strange that she is too busy to have dinner with us? Why is she being so secretive?"

"I don't know, Berry," Dash said. "She hasn't been home in a while, so maybe she has family to see. Besides, she is coming with us to look for Carobee tomorrow."

"Hmmmm," Berry said. She took a bite of a fresh white meringue. "Tomorrow can't come soon enough." And she thought, *Maybe I'll discover what Fruli's hiding.*

6

Sticky, Gooey Secret

Berry woke up early the next morning. She flew to Fruli's and found her five friends all in one room and fast asleep. Berry pushed open the windows and woke them up. She wanted to find Carobee, but she also needed to study patterns.

"Wake up, sleepy wings!" she cried. As

she flew around to each fairy, she noticed a vanilla-colored envelope on the center table. "Look, I have a note," Berry said.

"I wonder who it's from," Raina said.

"What does the note say?" Cocoa asked.

Berry read the letter out loud to her friends. "It's from Fruli. 'Sorry I had to fly off this morning. Ring the bell for breakfast. Puff will be by early to take you to look for Carobee. Send me a sugar fly note when you find him.'" Berry looked confused.

"I thought she was coming with us to find Carobee."

"She didn't mention why she had to leave so early," Dash said.

"No, she didn't," Berry said. "This is very suspicious, right?"

"Oh, Berry," Melli said. "You are being very hard on Fruli. She has been so kind to us and a good friend to you."

"I know," Berry admitted. She held the letter tightly in her hand. "But I just know she is keeping a secret! I hate secrets!"

"Just when you don't know the secret," Cocoa mumbled.

"Oh look, Puff is here to take us," Melli said, pointing out to the balcony. The large cream-colored unicorn was waiting for the

Candy Fairies there. Berry realized that Melli was trying to distract her. Her caramel friend didn't like when any of them got angry at one another. But Berry wasn't angry. She was frustrated!

The five friends mounted the unicorn and flew over the cliffs where Carobee lived. The dragon lived in the Candy Cliffs in Sugar Cove. There were many caves stuck into the large mountain in the cove, and Sprinkle Sands Beach was at the bottom. The beach was made of rainbow sprinkles and glistened in the sun.

"Look at all the caramel turtles," Melli said, pointing down at the beach.

"But no Carobee," Berry said. They flew up and down, searching the caves.

"It's a good thing we have Puff," Dash said. "This would have taken all day if we were flying on our own!"

"We never would have been able to cover all this area," Raina said. She searched down below. "Where could Carobee be?"

Berry sighed. "And I don't have much time," she told her friends. "I need to get to Sweet Stitches to set up my workstation. If only we could find Carobee!"

"Maybe we should check his cave," Cocoa said. "I know that seems too obvious, but maybe Carobee is there."

"If he was in his cave," Melli said, "he would have gotten our sugar fly note."

"Maybe he did and he didn't respond," Raina said softly.

Dash nodded. "It is worth a try. Remember, we found him in his cave when we first met him."

"All the more reason to check," she said. Berry inched up to whisper directions into Puff's ear.

The five fairies flew to the cave where they had first spotted the green-and-purple dragon with blue spots. At that time, they had thought Carobee was mean and melting all the candy in Sugar Valley. They had been very wrong about Carobee. Berry hoped Cocoa's hunch was right and the dragon was hiding out in his own cave.

As they neared the cave Berry let out a squeal. "I see Carobee's tail!"

Curling out of the cave was Carobee's

blue-spotted tail. The fairies flew off the unicorn and stood at the entrance.

"Carobee?" Berry called gently.

"Who is there?" a voice responded. When his head poked out of the cave, Carobee burst into tears.

"Are you hurt?" Dash asked.

"What's wrong?" Melli gasped.

"I'm so happy to see you," the dragon said. He snuffled and then blew out a strong gust of hot air. The five fairies were lifted off their feet. "Oh, I am sorry," he said. "I'm just so happy to see you."

"Then why are you crying?" Dash asked.

Carobee snuffled again. "These are happy tears," he said.

"Carobee, we were so worried when you

didn't answer our sugar fly note," Raina said. "What is going on?"

The dragon hung his large head. "I can't tell you," he said.

"*Another* secret?" Berry moaned.

Raina shot her a hard look. "Don't scare him, Berry," she scolded.

Berry took a deep breath. "Carobee, we're here to help you," she said. She watched the dragon close and open his eyes. It seemed like it took forever for Carobee to reply.

"I have done something terrible!" he wailed.

The five fairies looked at one another. They weren't sure what to make of Carobee's announcement.

"Is anyone hurt?" Raina asked bravely.

Carobee shook his head. "No, no one is

hurt. But I am in big, big trouble. Sticky, gooey trouble."

Again the fairies all shared a worried look.

"Let us help you," Cocoa said. "We came all this way to help."

Berry inched closer to Carobee. "Friends shouldn't keep secrets from one another. Maybe there is something we can do."

"I'm just so embarrassed," Carobee moaned. "How could I do such a thing?" He glanced up at the Candy Fairies. "I was supposed to deliver barrels of my fire-spun cotton-candy material to Olivia Crème de la Crème. I wasn't careful enough. I accidentally scorched and burned the entire batch!" He buried his head under his long leg. "I don't know what to say to Olivia Crème de la Crème.

What am I going to do? I have never been so embarrassed."

The Candy Fairies were shocked by Carobee's confession. They didn't know what to say.

Berry stepped forward. "Olivia will understand," she said.

"All those yards of cotton candy spun into fabric, ruined with one breath!" Carobee burst out.

"We can help you make up a new batch," Cocoa said brightly. "We are Candy Fairies, you know!"

Berry looked over at Raina. She knew her friend was thinking the same thing: there could only be one explanation for why there was so much cotton-candy material requested for Sweet Stitches. Berry's hand flew to her mouth. "The surprise competition fabric must be cotton candy!" she let out.

"Only there is no cotton-candy fabric," Dash noted. "Now that's a secret not worth finding out."

"But we can change that," Cocoa said. "Sure as sugar, we can get Carobee's order delivered if we work together."

Berry made a sour face. She wasn't sure if she should keep the surprise fabric news to herself, but she wanted to help Carobee. This was a sticky, gooey secret, just like Carobee said.

CHAPTER 7

Sugar Help

I can't believe I know the secret fabric!" Berry whispered back.

"Maybe there is another reason Olivia wants all that material," Raina said.

"Maybe," Berry agreed.

Berry's mind was racing. If she knew about the secret material ahead of everyone else, she would be cheating. But Berry loved making skirts out of cotton candy! Sure as sugar, she'd make a winning design with the gorgeous fabric. Razz would be extra-bitter about Berry's winning the grand prize! The thought made Berry grin. Then she looked over at Carobee. The dragon was looking so sad. Instantly she knew what was important.

"First we have to help Carobee," Berry said to Raina. "I will decide what to do later."

"You're right," Raina said, looking a little worried. "Though this is a pretty big cotton-candy secret."

"Come on," Berry said to Carobee. "We're not going to dip our wings in syrup! We can get started on some sugar for your new batch of cotton candy."

"There's still time, Carobee," Raina said.

"Don't give up," Cocoa added.

Carobee raised his head and blinked back his tears. "You are all so kind," he said. "I didn't think anyone could help me."

"You can always count on your friends," Berry told him. She hugged his neck and gave him a kiss on his cheek.

"Especially a Candy Fairy," Dash said. "We're friends till the end!"

The five Candy Fairies circled around a barrel, and soon it was filled with sweet, pink sugar. They filled a few more barrels and then stepped back.

"All ready for you," Berry said.

"Just fire the sugar up," Dash said.

Melli shot Dash a look. "Please be careful, Carobee," she said.

Carobee stood up and pushed the barrels

of freshly made Candy Fairy sugar out of his cave. He steadied his feet and lifted his head. "Here goes," he said.

Berry held her breath. She hoped Carobee would whip up the cotton candy as she had seen him do before.

The dragon's hot breath swirled the sugar into a tornado-shaped cone.

"So mint!" Dash exclaimed.

In minutes, next to the large barrels was a heap of cotton candy. The gorgeous pink was so delicious.

"Carobee!" Raina cried. "You did it!"

Carobee stood back and nuzzled the pile. "Now it needs to be woven into cloth," he said. "Can you help me load it into the loom?" His tail pointed back into his cave. "This can get a little sticky."

"Sure as sugar," Cocoa said, flying forward.

"If we all help, it will go faster," Berry said. "Which is good because I really need to get going."

The fairies worked together and wove the cotton candy into yards of soft pink material. Berry's fingers were itching to sew something with the scrumptious pink fabric!

As Berry watched Carobee work the loom she felt sad. She had so many ideas for designs using this material. She realized then how unfair her knowing about the fabric was to the other fairies, even Razz. Berry understood that part of the competition was being able to come up with a design quickly and on the spot.

"Remember, there is a chance that Olivia Crème de la Crème is using the material for something else," Raina said to her.

"Maybe," Berry said. "But now I have to fly. I have to get to Sweet Stitches to set up."

"We can't wait for the big show tonight," Melli said.

"And to see what you design," Cocoa added.

"Me too," Berry said, feeling her stomach flip-flop.

Raina pulled Berry aside. "What are you going to do?"

"I'm not sure," Berry admitted. "I think I should talk to Olivia." She glanced back to

Carobee. "But I don't want to get Carobee in any trouble."

Raina gave Berry a hug. "See you later," she said.

At Sweet Stitches, fairies were buzzing about what the surprise material might be. Berry didn't say a word. She set up her workspace and organized her needles and pins as Razz boasted to the others.

"Olivia will probably pick something challenging, like sugar lace," Razz said. "I am an expert at sewing that," she said.

"I hope it's chocolate roll," an Ice Cream Fairy said. "I just learned how to stitch up that material."

Razz made a face. "Oh, that wouldn't be

a challenge." She smirked. "I'm hoping for something really interesting and different."

Berry held her tongue. She wanted to blurt out her news, but she knew that wouldn't be smart. She flew up to one of the Sweet Stitches assistants. "I would like to speak to Olivia," Berry said.

"She won't be back until after lunch," the fairy replied.

Berry felt her heart start beating faster. "After lunch? Well, I—I guess . . . ," she stammered as she tried to think.

"Is this something urgent?" the fairy asked.

"What is so important, Berry?" Razz cried from across the room.

Berry had to cover for herself! She didn't

want to give her secret away. Especially not in front of Razz!

"Please tell Ms. Olivia that I need to speak to her before the competition begins and that I will be here after lunch," Berry said.

"Very well," the fairy said. "We'll see you later." She then turned her attention to the fairies setting up their sewing areas. She rang a small bell to get everyone's attention. "We are off to a good start!" She waved at all the work areas. "We will see you all tonight for the fashion event of the season!"

Berry raced out of the store. She didn't want to hear all of Razz's questions. She was not going to let Razz in on this secret. For her own sake—and for her friend Carobee's.

CHAPTER
8

Pure Honesty

At Fruli's house there was a large buffet spread out on the terrace overlooking Cone Harbor. Berry saw her friends piling up their plates with the colorful fresh treats. Berry was not hungry at all. She didn't know how she was going to confess to Olivia that she knew the big secret.

Carobee was the first to spot Berry when she arrived. He came over to her.

"I need to tell Olivia what happened," Carobee said. "I put you in a sticky spot. I'm very sorry."

Berry shook her head. "Don't be silly," she said. "It is my responsibility to come forward." She lowered her head. "I just don't know how to tell Olivia."

Carobee roared. "Just tell the truth," he said. "If I had been honest from the beginning, there would be no cotton-candy mess. Pure honesty is like pure sugar. I should have told Olivia about the batch burning when it happened."

Berry's friends flew around her. She was happy that they were all there with her.

81

"Being honest is hard, but it is the only way," Carobee said.

"Sure as sugar, there is only one thing to do, then," Berry said. "Carobee, please come with me to speak to Olivia after lunch."

"Now, that sounds like a grand plan!" Raina cried.

"As good as these meringue cookies," Dash said, stuffing her face.

Berry smiled. "Sweet strawberries! There is so much food here," she said, taking in the long tables and platters piled high with food.

"I think the staff knew that Dash was coming," Cocoa said, giggling.

"Very funny," Dash said. Then she smiled. "I do love a good buffet."

Suddenly Berry was very hungry. "Maybe

 82

I will have a little something before Carobee and I go to Sweet Stitches," she said.

Berry told her friends all about the other fairies and setting up the workstations for the competition. She explained how she had lined up all her needles and spools of thread. "I don't want to search for anything," Berry explained. "Every minute counts!"

"We can't wait to see Raina walk down the runway," Melli said.

"Me too!" Berry exclaimed. "I hope she likes her dress!"

"Oh, I'm sure it will be *sugar-tastic*," Raina said.

Berry finished her lunch. She felt better already. She may not have been sure about what to say to Olivia, but she knew it was the right thing to do. And Carobee's coming with her made her stronger.

"Good luck," Raina said to Berry. "But I don't think you'll need it. I think Olivia will understand."

"Thanks," Berry said. She gave her friends hugs. "And thank you again for being here."

"My pleasure!" Dash said, flying back up to the buffet table for another helping.

Berry flew up to Carobee's back, and the two of them headed to Sweet Stitches. The other contestants must have been out exploring the island, since no one was at the shop. Berry saw the fairy who had told her Olivia would be around after lunch.

"Excuse me," Berry said in her most polite voice. "We'd like to speak to Olivia."

The fairy did a double take when seeing Carobee. Berry knew that it wasn't every day a green-and-purple dragon was in the waiting room at the fancy dress shop.

"Have a seat," the fairy said. "I'll see if she is available."

When the fairy closed the door, Berry turned to Carobee. "I'm so nervous," she said.

"I know," Carobee said. "Let's just get this part over with so Olivia can decide what to do about the contest. Then you can get focused on designing the best dress you can sew!"

The door opened and Olivia flew into the room. She smelled like fresh vanilla sugar cookies.

"Hello, Berry," she said. Then she smiled at Carobee. "I see you have met Carobee." She petted Carobee's long snout. "Hello, friend," she said to him. "What brings both of you here?"

They must have seemed a funny pair to Olivia, Berry thought. Why would a Candy Fairy know Carobee?

"Carobee and I are old friends," Berry explained.

"And Berry and her friends were kind enough to help me out of a very difficult situation," Carobee said.

Olivia sat down on the couch and patted the cushion next to her. "Please come sit down," she said to Berry.

Carobee couldn't wait another second. "I burned the cotton-candy fabric that I was supposed to deliver," he blurted out.

Olivia looked confused. "But the order arrived this morning," she said, "and it looked scrumptious."

"Only because Berry and her Candy Fairy friends helped me make a new batch," the dragon said, hanging his head.

"Oh," Olivia said. "I think I understand." She turned to Berry.

"I had to tell you," Berry said. "I felt it would be cheating if I came tonight knowing the fabric for the competition *before* any of the other fairies."

Berry held her breath as Olivia flew up and circled the room.

"Thank you for coming forward," Olivia said. "It is very honest of you, and I appreciate honesty." She turned to look at Carobee.

"Are you okay? Were you hurt at all?"

Shaking his large head, Carobee sighed. "Just my pride, Ms. Crème de la Crème."

"I'm glad everyone is fine," she went on. "Berry, I will see that the fabric for the contest is changed so that you will be in the same position as the other eleven designers." She flew over to Berry. "Thank you," she continued. "Other fairies may not have come to tell me this story. I am glad you both did."

"Me too!" Berry exclaimed. She felt so much lighter. She flew up in the air and gave Carobee a tight squeeze. "Carobee encouraged me not to be afraid to tell you. And I am so glad that I listened."

Olivia smiled. "Yes, Carobee has good advice," she said. "And good taste! His fabrics are top-notch! Now, I've got some work to do. Please excuse me."

"Thank you," Berry said. "I'll see you later."

"Yes, I will see you both later," Olivia said. "At showtime!"

CHAPTER

9

Pure Pink

Berry and Carobee returned to Fruli's house. There wasn't much time before the contest, but Berry wanted to let her friends know how her talk with Olivia had gone. She felt so much better!

Before Berry and Carobee touched the ground, Raina guessed what had happened at Sweet Stitches.

"You told Olivia Crème de la Crème!" she cried. "You are both grinning, so I know the talk went fine."

"More than fine," Berry told her friends. She hopped off Carobee's back. "We had a *sugar-tastic* visit with Olivia."

"*Choc-o-rific!*" Cocoa said.

Carobee roared happily.

Berry noticed that Fruli was standing next to Cocoa.

"Hello," Fruli said. "Raina and the others were telling me what happened." She walked over to Carobee. "I'm so sorry you were feeling sad. I wish I had known. I would have helped. Please ask me next time something so sour happens."

Carobee bowed his head. "Thank you, Fruli."

Berry noticed that Fruli was writing on a

small pad of paper with a chocolate pencil.

"What are you doing, Fruli? Are you taking *notes?*" Berry asked. She narrowed her eyes. "What are you up to?"

Fruli smiled. "Well, I can finally tell you now," she said.

Berry's eyes widened. "So you *were* keeping a secret!" she exclaimed.

"Not really a secret," Fruli said. She winked at Raina.

Noticing that her friends were smiling at one another, Berry was getting juiced up. "*Everyone* knows?" she asked.

Raina put her hand on Berry's shoulder. "Calm down," she said. "Fruli just told us."

"You see," Fruli said to Berry, "I was feeling very jealous of you."

"What?" Berry asked. "Why were you jealous of me?"

Raina nudged Berry. "Listen," she told her.

"When the fashion design contestants were announced, you were so sure about being a part of it," Fruli said. "Your designs got you invited. I was invited because of my family. I can't design clothes like you, Berry. I love fashion and clothes, but I couldn't sew two strips of material together!"

"You can sew," Berry said.

"No, I can't," Fruli said. "Fairy's promise." She crossed her heart with her finger. "My clothes are made for me. I wish that I could design and sew like you, Berry! Princess Lolli saw me the morning that the invitations went out. She understood why I didn't want to accept, and she came up with a *sweet-tacular* idea."

Berry was so stunned about Fruli's being jealous of her that she was having a hard time following Fruli's story. Berry was the one who felt jealous of Fruli!

"I am going to write about fashion in the *Daily Scoop*!" Fruli exclaimed. "Princess Lolli has been very helpful and introduced me to the *Daily Scoop* editor." Fruli flew over, closer to Berry. "My first article is going to be about you, Berry! I wanted it to be a surprise."

"Me?" Berry asked. She sat down on a white meringue puff stool.

"Yes!" Fruli said. "You are a great story."

"A great story would be if I win the design show," Berry told her.

Fruli laughed. "Not necessarily," she said.

 95

"At first I was going to write about how you've always wanted to be in the contest and how hard you've worked to practice and learn all you could. Then when Carobee's problem was discovered, you shone even brighter. You were honest and came forward about the secret fabric, and you were there to help a friend. This is all great material for my first report as fashion editor!"

"Oh, Fruli, you are so sweet," Berry said. She stood up to face her friend. "No one knows more about fashion than you. You are going to be a *sugar-tastic* fashion

editor." She gave her friend a tight squeeze. "Now I feel terrible that I was so jealous of you!"

Fruli took a step back. "Jealous of me?" She laughed. "I am the one who should be jealous. Especially of the great dress that I know you will design today."

Berry grinned. "Thank you. I'm glad that now there are no more secrets between us."

"Me too," Fruli replied.

"We'd better get going," Melli said, looking up at the clock on the wall. "Berry, it is almost time for the contest to start."

Raina shook her wings. "I'm getting nervous now!"

"Don't worry," Cocoa told her. "After being a gumdrop for Princess Lolli, this walk will be a piece of chocolate!"

"And definitely as sweet," Raina said, smiling.

The fairies rode Puff to Sweet Stitches, with Carobee close behind. Berry said good-bye to her friends and showed Raina where her workstation was located in the large tent behind the store.

"Sweet sugar!" Raina exclaimed when she saw Berry's work area. "You are so organized!"

Berry stood back and admired the rows of thread spools and all her needles lined up. She was glad she had spent time making her station neat. Now if only Olivia would announce the fabric! She had so many ideas!

"I heard your friend Carobee had a little problem," Razz said as she flew above Berry and Raina.

Berry knew better than to answer. She just

looked up at Razz. "Good luck, Razz," she said. "I hope you have a good show."

Razz's face puckered up tight, as if she'd had the sourest lemon drop in Sour Orchard. She spun around and flew over to her workstation.

"Ha!" Raina exclaimed. "You got her with some sugar!"

"I've learned that the best way to deal with Razz is with some sweetness," Berry said. She laughed, feeling relieved that Razz was on the other side of the tent.

Just then Olivia Crème de la Crème flew to the stage. "Welcome to the Meringue Island Fashion Show for Young Fairies," she said. "The fabric for today's design is"—she looked over at Berry—"a cotton-candy-colored sugar weave."

There was a cheer from all the contestants, but Berry was the one who cheered the loudest. "Now the contest is truly fair," she whispered to Raina. "Even though it is the same pretty color as cotton candy, the fabric is completely different."

The material for the contest was placed at Berry's table. Berry loved the color, and the material was soft and smooth. "Leave it to Olivia Crème de la Crème to pick the perfect fabric for all the fairies to design with!" Berry said happily. "And to make this contest fair and lemon square!"

"It is gorgeous!" Raina said. "Pure pink!"

Berry started sketching and imagining how she would drape the fabric. She was grateful that Raina was her model. It was nice to have her friend nearby. In a flash, she had a great idea how to show off the flowing fabric. She would make layers for the skirt of the dress so the fabric would swirl around Raina as she walked. Then she thought to make a wide sugarcoated belt around the waist. She had so many thoughts! It was hard for her fingers to keep up!

As she worked Berry glanced over at her friends. Fruli was writing in her notebook, Melli and Cocoa were reading the design booklet about each of the contestants, and Dash was munching on meringues.

Berry felt as lucky as a first-place winner already.

10

Sweet Surprise

Berry turned the pink dress around for Raina to see. Then she held her breath as Raina slipped her new design on.

"Oh, Berry!" Raina exclaimed. She looked at herself in the mirror. "Sweet sugar! The dress is *sugar-tastic*! And it fits me perfectly."

"Hold on," Berry said. "I'm not finished yet!

I have one more thing to do. Slip it off again."

From her pocket, Berry took out a small pouch. "There are no rules against using these," she said. She poured a few of her precious sugarcoated fruit chews into her hand. "This will be the sweetest trim for the dress."

She carefully sewed the sparkling fruit chews on the dress. Then she stood back and handed the dress to Raina. "You will rock it on the runway," Berry told her friend.

"Sure as sugar!" Raina said, smiling. She put the dress on and spun around. "I love it!"

Just then a horn sounded and the designers had to finish up their dresses. The show was about to start! There were many fairies flying about and lots of chatter as everyone got ready. Berry was relieved that she had finished on time. Some fairies were still sewing as their models lined up for the walk!

Berry saw that Razz had made a miniskirt and top out of the fabric. Her lines and sewing were top-notch. She was one of the fairies Berry would need to beat.

"Good luck," Berry said to Razz.

"You too," Razz replied.

For the first time, Berry noticed that Razz seemed nervous. Razz didn't make one of her usual sour remarks. Berry shared a smile with Razz, one designer to another. They were both nervous before the show.

Berry and Raina peered out from behind the curtain and saw the long runway.

"That is a long, long walk," Raina said.

"Remember, you walk down to the end and turn. Then when you come back, I come out and walk with you," Berry whispered.

"I'm glad you get to walk with me," Raina said. "That way everyone will get to see the designer of this *sugar-tastic* dress."

"Let's hope everyone thinks the dress is so *sugar-tastic*," Berry said just as the music started.

Backstage, Olivia Crème de la Crème clapped her hands. "Attention, models and designers!" she said. "Good luck to all of you. You have all done a scrumptious job. Now the show will begin! Wait for your cues, and I will see you on the runway!" She flew out through the center curtain. She headed down the runway to greet the guests and to take her place at the judges' table.

Berry peered out and saw all the fairies. She spotted the judges' table. She saw the four designers sitting there with scorecards, and her heart skipped a few beats. Those four designers were Meringue Island's top fashion designers! And they would be judging her dress!

"Berry! Berry! Berry!"

Berry saw Dash, in a corner by the stage, waving her hands. She was flying above the crowd, trying to get her attention. Berry smiled. It was supersweet to have her friends nearby. Berry watched a few models and designers fly down the runway.

"We're next!" Raina said, tugging at Berry's hand.

Berry took a deep breath. "Thanks, Raina. You are the most beautiful model."

"And this is the most delicious dress," Raina told her. She spun around. "Here I go!"

Berry held her breath as Raina flew down the runway. The white tent was glowing with lights, and Raina floated down the long stage, the dress flowing behind her. She was so graceful. Berry was proud. She noticed how the judges wrote down comments but none of them smiled.

"Your turn," Raina said. She reached out for Berry's hand and guided her on stage.

The lights were bright, and Berry heard the crowd cheer. She held Raina's hand tightly. e was excited and nervous both at the same

When they returned to the curtain, they both took a bow. Then they went to the side of the stage as another fairy flew down the runway.

"That was *sugar-tastic*!" Raina exclaimed. "Did you hear all those cheers?"

Berry nodded. "As Dash would say, that was *so mint*!"

Raina laughed. "Now we have to wait," she said. "Come, let's sit over here so we can watch the others." She flew to the side of the stage.

All the dresses were different styles, and Berry was amazed by how each fairy had used material. Judging this contest was not be easy.

last fairy exited the runway, la Crème came out onto the

stage. "While the judges are reviewing their comments, we have a sweet surprise for you all." She looked off to the side of the stage. "I'd like to welcome my dear friends Char, Carob, and Chip."

"The Sugar Pops are here?!" Raina squealed.

The crowd roared with delight as the music group walked onstage.

Berry and all the fairies loved the music group the Sugar Pops. The three brothers were supersweet, and their music was everyone's favorite.

"Melli, Cocoa, and Dash are so happy right now," Berry said. She giggled. "Me too!"

Everyone sang along to "Yum Pop," the group's most famous song. After the brother sang a few more tunes, Berry saw C collecting the judges' comments. It was time for the winner to be announced!

Olivia flew to the center of the stage. "Thank you, Sugar Pops," she said. "And a huge thank-you to all the judges and to my Sweet Stitches staff. This was one of the most memorable design shows. I would like a round of applause for all the designers. This show was a big challenge, and all of them were excellent. They made this decision very difficult."

The twelve contestants and their models stood together backstage. Berry squeezed Raina's hand. She couldn't wait to hear!

"The design award this year goes to . . .

~y the Fruit Fairy!" Olivia announced.

v had hoped Olivia would say her

name, but she couldn't believe her name was called! She was a frozen fruit stick, not able to move!

"Berry! That's you!" Raina cried. She pushed Berry forward.

Berry flew over to Olivia at the end of the long runway.

"Maybe you'll come work for me one day," Olivia said to her. "Your work shows creativity and great use of color. I love how you've added your sugarcoated gems and made this design uniquely yours. And you have proved that you are honest and a good friend. Bravo!"

Berry felt as if she would burst with happiness! "Thank you," she said. She cradled the award in her arms.

"Good work," Razz said to Berry when she returned backstage.

"Thank you," Berry said. "You did good work too."

"Berry," Fruli called, "well done! My article will be even sweeter now!"

Berry smiled. "Thanks," she said. "I can't wait to read it, Fruli."

The crowd cheered again, and Berry took Raina's hand to go stand out on the runway together once more. Berry looked over to see her friends jumping around. She wanted to savor the sweet moment. It was the sweetest victory. And that was no secret!

Candy Fairies

Chocolate Dreams   Rainbow Swirl   Caramel Moon   Cool Mint   Magic Hearts   Gooey Goblins

The Sugar Ball   A Valentine's Surprise   Bubble Gum Rescue   Double Dip   Jelly Bean Jumble   The Chocolate Rose

A Royal Wedding   Marshmallow Mystery   Frozen Treats   The Sugar Cup   Sweet Secrets   Taffy Trouble

Visit candyfairies.com for games, recipes, and more!